Tom Sawyer

Retold by
Saviour Pirotta

Illustrated by
Vince Reid

ARCTURUS

For Albie Paton—SP.

For Pat and Mary—VR.

ARCTURUS

This edition published in 2018 by Arcturus Publishing Limited
26/27 Bickels Yard, 151–153 Bermondsey Street,
London SE1 3HA

Writer: Saviour Pirotta
Illustrator: Vince Reid
Designer: Jeni Child
Editor: Sebastian Rydberg
Art Director: Jessica Crass

ISBN: 978-1-78828-694-7
CH006285NT
Supplier 24, Date 0318, Print run 6735

Printed in Malaysia

Contents

CHAPTER 1

Painting the Fence

"It's not fair," groaned Tom Sawyer, coming out of the house with a paintbrush. His aunt Polly followed with a bucket of whitewash.

"That'll teach you to skip school, Tom," she said.

"And to lie," added Tom's cousin Mary. She had come out behind Aunt Polly.

"I promised your mother before she died that I'd look after you and your brother, Sid," said Aunt Polly. "And that includes teaching you to obey your elders."

"And to tell the truth," giggled Mary.

It was a mighty warm Saturday. All the children in St. Petersburg would be going down to the river to swim. But not Tom. He had to paint the garden fence as punishment for skipping school.

The front door banged shut behind Aunt Polly and Cousin Mary. Tom's heart sank. The fence was big. He would never finish painting it by the end of the day, let alone in time for a swim.

He'd have to get help. Perhaps he could pay some of his friends to do some whitewashing. Tom emptied his pockets to see what he could pay them with. He had only a couple of marbles and a few bits of string.

The situation seemed hopeless, until
he had the best idea ever! The first boy
to come past the house was his friend
Ben Rogers, pretending to be a grand
steamboat. He was taking bites out of a
big, juicy apple in between the tooting.

"You coming along for a swim, Tom?"

Tom picked up the brush and started
painting. "Who'd want to go swimming

when they have a lovely
fence to whitewash?"

"You mean you
choose to stay home
and work?" cried Ben.

"It's only work if you
don't want to do it!"

Ben stared at the fence. "Please, Tom,
could I have a go?"

Tom sloshed more whitewash on the

fence. "Not sure you'll do a good job, Ben."

"I'll give you what's left of my apple," pleaded Ben.

"Alright," said Tom at last. He sat down on the grass and took a big bite out of Ben's apple. His trick had worked. Here he was, resting in the sun while Ben did all the hard work. Another friend, Johnny Miller, came along. He, too, wanted to have a go at painting. Tom wouldn't let him till he handed over his kite.

Before long, there was a long line of children wanting to help paint the fence. By the time it was finished, Tom had a collection of goodies, including marbles, toys, and even a dead rat swinging on a piece of string.

Tom learned a great lesson that warm, sunny day. If you want to sell something to people, make it hard to get. Then everyone will want it.

He went in to ask Aunt Polly if he could go swimming. She was so astonished to see the fence all painted, she gave him another apple.

Coming home
from the river later
that evening, Tom
spotted a girl in Judge
Thatcher's garden across
the street. She was picking
flowers. He'd never seen
her before.

"Hello," called Tom.

The girl ignored him. Tom did some
cartwheels to impress her. She still didn't
look his way. Instead, she threw a pansy
over her shoulder and went indoors.
Tom's heart beat like a drum. That girl
was the prettiest he'd ever seen. She
was even prettier than Amy Lawrence at
school. Tom was in love with Amy. Or had
been till now. Now, Tom's heart belonged
only to this mysterious girl.

He pounced on the pansy and held it
close. He would keep it till the day he died.

Next morning, Tom got to school late.

"Thomas Sawyer," cried Mr. Dobbins,
the schoolmaster. "What kept you?"

Tom was about to make an excuse
involving Aunt Polly. Then, he spotted
the mysterious girl. She was sitting
with the other girls on their side of the
schoolroom, an empty chair at her desk.
Tom saw an opportunity …

"I got held up chatting to Huckleberry Finn, sir," he replied.

Mr. Dobbin's face turned a bright purple. "You did what, Thomas Sawyer?"

Huckleberry Finn was a street urchin, the son of a drunk. He slept outdoors and had been caught stealing. All adults considered him a very bad example.

"You were told not to talk to Master Finn," growled Mr. Dobbins, reaching for his cane. "Take off your jacket, Thomas."

Later, Tom sat down with his bottom stinging. His friends tittered, but he ignored them. His plan had worked. He'd been made to sit on the girls' side, right next to the mysterious girl. She seemed to feel sorry for Tom. "Hello," she said.

Tom's heart leaped for joy. She'd spoken to him!

He placed a peach in front of her. "Pleese, tejk it," he scrawled on his slate.

"I'm Becky," she whispered. "My father's Judge Thatcher. I've just moved here."

Tom scrawled *I love you* on his slate.

"You bad thing," giggled Becky.

At dinner time, Tom and Becky sat on the grass. "Do you like ice cream, Becky?"

"I love it so," answered Becky.

Tom fished a brass paperweight from his pocket. "I don't have money for ice cream," he said. "But I will one day, I promise.

Meanwhile, here's a gift for you."

He watched Becky admiring it. "Becky, was you ever engaged?"

"Engaged?" said Becky.

"You know, to be married," said Tom. "Do you love me enough to marry me?"

"I do! But how do you get engaged?"

"Why, you just kiss."

"Well, I'll close my eyes, and we'll kiss," said Becky, and they kissed. "Now you must never marry anyone but me, Tom."

"And you must never choose anyone for games at parties but me," said Tom. "Why, when Amy and I were engaged ..."

Becky's eyes grew wide with horror. "You've been engaged before?"

"I don't love Amy any longer," said Tom hurriedly. "I only love you, Becky." But it was too late. Becky had stomped off.

CHAPTER 2

Ghosts in the Graveyard

Tom decided to skip school for the afternoon. He wandered down to the river, where he ran into Huckleberry Finn carrying a dead cat by the tail.

"I'm using it to get rid of the warts on my hand," he explained.

"Say," Tom said. "How do you do that?"

"Why, you takes it to the graveyard at night," explained Huck. "You stand close to a grave where someone wicked has just been buried. At night, the devil will come to fetch the wicked man's soul to hell. You throws the cat after the devil and say: 'Devil follow corpse, cat follow devil, warts follow cat, I'm done with ye.' And the warts will leap straight off you and follow the devil to hell. I'm going to the graveyard tonight. Old Hoss Williams has just been buried, and I reckons he was a very wicked man. Wanna come with me?"

Tom could not possibly say no. He might never get the chance to see warts jumping off someone again.

"I'll fetch ye tonight," Huck promised.

Time passed very slowly as Tom waited for Huck in his room.

At last, he heard a loud howling on the street below. It sounded like a cat, but Tom knew it wasn't. It was Huckleberry Finn, sending a signal.

Tom howled back to show he'd heard. Then, he climbed out of the window. Soon, the two boys were in the graveyard.

The wind moaned in the trees. It sounded like a ghost, looking for its grave.

"I reckons the devil is about tonight," whispered Huck.

Tom spotted a faint light hovering at the other end of the graveyard. "Huck," he gasped. "The devil is about. Look, he's coming."

Both boys dived behind a tree, their hearts beating loudly. "Think the devil'll get us?" cried Huck, "Pray, Tom, pray."

Tom began to pray. But then he

stopped. A muffled voice carried on the wind. And he recognized it.

"Why, Huck, that ain't no devil. That's old, drunk Muff Potter with the lantern. And there's two more fellas with him."

Tom and Huck watched from behind the tree as Muff and his two pals came closer. They stopped by Hoss's grave, only a few feet away from the boys. Muff put down the lantern.

"I know the other two," muttered Huck. "One's that old crook, Injun Joe. The other's Dr. Robinson, the doctor."

Muff and Injun Joe started digging. Soon, they had uncovered Hoss's coffin.

"Bring up the corpse, hurry!" barked Dr. Robinson.

"Not so fast, doctor," replied Muff. "Injun Jo and I want another five each."

"Muff's right," growled Injun Joe. "If you want this body for your experiments, you're going to have to pay more, Doctor."

"No, I've paid you enough," said Dr. Robinson firmly.

"Why …" hissed Injun Jo, grabbing Dr. Robinson by the collar. "Five years ago, I came to your house begging for bread. You had me thrown in jail for breaking into your garden. I swore then

I'd have my revenge. So pay up, or I'll crush your head with my bare hands."

Dr. Robinson kicked out with his leg and sent Injun Jo flying.

"Hey," said Muff, clambering out of the grave. "You leave my friend alone." He tried to grab Dr. Robinson, too, but the doctor pushed over the gravestone. It landed on Muff's head with a loud thud. The drunk was knocked out cold. "Why, you …" roared Injun Joe. He spotted Muff's knife sticking out from under his belt. He snatched it and plunged it in Dr. Robinson's chest.

Just then, the moon slid behind a cloud. When it came out again, Dr. Robinson was lying on the ground in a pool of blood. Muff was sitting up. He looked dazed. The knife was in his hands.

"Muff, you shouldn't drink so much," said Injun Joe. "Now, see—you've gone and killed Dr. Robinson. Let's get away from here, quick."

The two men hurried away. Tom and Huck stared at Dr. Robinson's corpse. Their hair stood on end. Then, they stood up and ran away as fast as they could.

"We got to tell Judge Thatcher what we saw," said Tom. "Injun Joe is pinning the murder on poor Muff Potter."

"We cain't do that," said Huck. "Injun Joe'll be after us. We have to swear never to say anything about this to anyone."

"Alright," said Tom. "I swear."

"That ain't enough for this kind of promise," said Huck. "We have to write an oath. We have to seal the deal with blood."

They found a flat stone by the roadside. Tom took a piece of chalk from his pocket and started writing:

Huck Finn and Tom Sawyer swears they will keep mum about this, and they wish they may drop down dead in their tracks if they ever tell and rot.

Then, they both pricked their thumb with a pin from Tom's pocket and signed their name in blood. They buried the flat stone deep in the ground, where no one would ever find it.

In the morning, as Tom was getting dressed, something came flying through the window. It landed on the carpet with a thud. Becky had returned the brass paperweight he had given her as a gift!

Tom went down to breakfast with a heavy heart. Nothing in his life seemed to be working.

"Tom, something awful happened," said Cousin Mary. "Poor old Muff Potter has been arrested for the murder of Dr. Robinson."

CHAPTER 3

An Island and a Funeral

Tom's heart was broken over Becky returning the paperweight. He was scared Injun Jo might find out he and Huck had seen his crime. There was nothing for it. Tom decided to run away. He would go that very night, while everyone was sleeping.

On his way to school, Tom met his friend, Joe Harper. He looked sad, too. "My ma's accused me of eating the cream," said Joe. "I'm planning on running away."

"Me, too," cried Tom. "No one loves me. I might turn pirate or soldier."

"I had my mind set on becoming a hermit," said Joe, "but I'll go with you instead, Tom."

"I'll ask Huckleberry Finn to come with us," added Tom. "He's the best person I know at running away."

At midnight, the three boys met at a secret spot on the riverbank. Tom brought a large ham. Joe had an enormous side of bacon. Huck had stolen a frying pan to cook the meat on. They found an old raft and sailed to an island in the middle of the river.

It was called Jackson's Island, and it was full of trees. No one lived on it. It was the perfect hiding place.

"We shall live here til we die," said Tom.

"Yeah," agreed Joe, "I shall never return to civilization."

They fried some delicious ham and bacon. Then, they stretched out on the grass to sleep. Tom looked up at the stars, feeling very contented. There was no Aunt Polly to tell him off now. No Becky to break his heart. And no Injun Joe to try and murder him. He fell asleep and had wonderful dreams.

In the morning, the boys discovered that the raft had floated away. Not that it mattered. They didn't need it anymore.

They spent the morning fishing and swimming. Coming back to their camp at lunchtime, they spied a ferryboat moored across the river. There were people on the deck, scurrying about.

Little fishing boats were sailing around it.

"Whatever is going on?" wondered Tom, peeping through a bush.

"They're looking for something," said Tom, craning his neck.

Suddenly, there was a loud puff of smoke on the ferry. It was followed by a loud "boom," and a cannonball shot across the water.

"Why," cried Huck. "I believes they're looking for a drowned body."

"How does a cannonball find a drowned body?" Joe wanted to know.

"It churns up the water so the body floats to the surface," replied Huck. "I seen it happen when old Bill Turner got drowned last year."

"Wonder who drowned this year."

Tom grinned from ear to ear. "Us, Joe. Someone must have found our raft and think we drowned."

Suddenly, Tom felt a lump in his throat. People did love him if they were looking for him. He wondered how Aunt Polly, Sid, and Mary were taking the news.

That night, after Huck and Joe had gone to sleep, Tom swam across the river. Soon, he was crouching outside Aunt

Polly's living room. He took a peep inside.
Aunt Polly sat with Sid, Mary, and Joe's
mother. They were all dressed in black.

"Those poor children," wailed Aunt
Polly. "Tom was such a lovely boy. He was
naughty, but he had a heart of gold. He
was my rock. I depended on him."

My rock! Tom had never heard Aunt
Polly call him that before. His chest
swelled with pride.

"We shall give all three boys a splendid funeral service on Sunday," howled Aunt Polly.

"And a mighty fine funeral it will be, even if the coffins are empty," sobbed Joe's mother.

"Amen," sobbed Mary and Sid.

When Aunt Polly blew out the lamp, Tom hurried back to Jackson's Island. In the morning, he told Joe and Huck all about the wonderful funeral they were to have.

"I didn't know we were so loved," said Joe. "It almost makes me wish I could go back there."

On Sunday, everyone in St. Petersburg was crammed into church. Three small coffins lay in front of the altar. The air was full of sobbing and the rustling of

mourning clothes.

Mr. Sprague, the minister, began the sermon. He talked about Tom and Joe and Huck. He told stories that showed how brave and kind they were.

"Yes, sir, they were wonderful boys," cried Mr. Dobbins.

"Always kind to old ladies," bawled Widow Douglas, the richest woman in the whole town.

Suddenly, there was the sound of sobbing up in the church gallery. Footsteps echoed down the wooden stairs. Everyone turned to see three boys walking up the aisle. It was Tom and Joe and Huckleberry Finn. They had sneaked into the church to attend their own funeral.

"Ha," bawled Joe. "You're all so kind about us, we're moved to tears."

"Why, my Joe is back from the dead,"

shrieked Mrs. Harper.

"And so is our Tom," cried Mary. "Thank the good Lord."

"And Huck," said Tom, "Don't forget Huck. He's safe and sound, too."

Everyone gathered around the boys. "We're mighty relieved to see you still in the land of the living," said Mr. Dobbins.

Tom thought how nice it was to be back home. To know that he had been missed by everyone in town. Only one person didn't seem glad to see him.

Becky Thatcher was frowning at him from the front pew.

CHAPTER 4

Under the Cross

Tom tried very hard to make friends with Becky again. She would have none of it. "I'll ask you to keep yourself to yourself, Thomas Sawyer," she snapped, when he tried to talk to her in the schoolyard. "I'm never going to be engaged to you again."

The situation seemed hopeless until a few days later.

Mr. Dobbins had a book that he kept locked in his desk. He took it out only once every day to read while the class were doing arithmetic. No one in school had ever looked in it or knew what it was about.

Then one lunchtime, Mr. Dobbins went out for a walk. Becky found herself alone in the schoolroom. Everyone else had gone outside to play. She noticed that Mr. Dobbins had left the key in the desk drawer. Quick as a flash, she took out the book and opened the cover.

"Oh," she cried. "It's a book of anatomy."

She gazed in wonder at a huge picture showing the insides of a human body. Just then, Tom came in looking for her. Becky tried snapping the book shut. She did it in such a hurry, she ripped the picture of the human body in two.

"See what you made me do, Tom, you horrible thing," she cried. "Don't you know you should never sneak up on a girl?" She put the book back in the desk and turned the key.

Later that afternoon, Mr. Dobbins took out his precious book to look at. He gasped when he found the torn picture.

"Who has ripped up my book?" he growled. "Joe Harper, was it you? Or you, Alfred Temple?" Tom could see Becky trembling with fear. She was trying to raise her hand, but she couldn't. He leaped instantly to his feet.

"I did it, sir."

"Come here this instant, Thomas Sawyer!" hissed Mr. Dobbins. Tom knew what was coming. A whipping. His bottom was stinging when he left school after a two-hour detention. But the pain didn't matter. He had saved his dear Becky from a severe punishment. And she was extremely grateful.

"Oh, Tom," she said the next morning. "How could you be so noble? You're a real hero."

With Becky his best friend again, Tom should have been happy. But he wasn't. He was anxious and worried. Muff Potter's trial was coming up. The poor man might be hanged for a crime he did not commit.

And it would be Tom and Huck's fault because they were too scared to tell what they had seen.

The boys went to see Muff in prison. They took him some food.

"You've been mighty good to me, boys," said Muff. "Better than anyone else in this town."

That made Tom feel even more guilty. "Are you sure we can't tell anyone what really happened that night?" he asked Huck.

"Injun Joe or one of his friends will kill us for sure," replied Huck. "We have to keep our secret whatever happens."

The trial started. All of St. Petersburg came to watch, even Injun Joe. Muff Potter was brought to the dock. Judge Thatcher took his seat.

He called one witness after another.
One said that he saw Muff sharpening
his knife on the day of the murder.
Another claimed he had spotted Muff
sneaking into the graveyard on the night
of the murder. An old woman said she
had come across Muff washing himself in
a stream the same night. The water
around him was red with blood.

Muff looked terrified as the witnesses spoke, but Injun Joe seemed pleased. He kept chuckling to himself. Somehow, he looked even more terrifying when he was smiling. But Tom just couldn't live with his guilt. He leaped off his seat and shouted, "Mr. Judge, sir, Muff Potter is innocent. Injun Joe did it. Huckleberry Finn and I saw everything."

There were screams at the back of the courtroom as Injun Joe jumped to his feet. He pushed his way roughly through the crowds. In a moment, he had crashed through the window.

Muff Potter was saved, and Tom was the hero of St. Petersburg. The local

paper even said he might be president of
the United States one day.

Once again, Tom should have been
happy. But he couldn't stop thinking
about Injun Joe. People said they'd seen
him leave town on the morning train.
But what if they were wrong? What if
Injun Joe came back at night to get his
revenge on Tom? Tom
was so terrified,
he couldn't
sleep at night.

"There's nothing
for it, Huck," Tom
said. "We've got to
do something to take
our mind off things."

"Like what?"
said Huck.

"We could look for treasure," Tom said.

"Ha," said Huck. "That's bully. I likes that idea. But where will we dig?"

"Somewhere spooky," said Tom. "That's where robbers always hide their treasure. It stops folk from coming to look for it."

"I knows a spooky place," cried Huck. "The deserted house on Cardiff Hill. It's haunted. Come on, Tom, let's borrow your aunt's shovel."

The two boys made their way to the house on Cardiff Hill. It was indeed very spooky and dark. Enormous cobwebs hung from the ceiling in every room. The floorboards creaked.

"Let's see what's upstairs," said Huck. "Someone might've left some old clothes behind. I could do with a spare shirt."

They were halfway up the stairs when

they heard voices. "Ghosts," gasped Tom.

"Don't be silly," said Huck. "It's people, and they're alive."

They ran up the rest of the stairs and hid in a bedroom. It was dusty, and there was a big hole in the floorboards. Tom and Huck could see right through it to the kitchen below. The voices got louder, and two men came in.

One of them was a Spanish man in a poncho. The other was—Injun Joe. So, he hadn't skipped town after all. Tom felt his blood turn cold.

"You sure there's a treasure in this house?" said the Spanish man.

"That's what I heard," replied Injun Joe. "The Murrel gang buried it here after they robbed a train."

The two men pried up the floorboards to reveal a hole in the floor. They pulled out a wooden chest. Injun Joe smashed the lock with the shovel Huck had left on the floor. The Spanish man threw back the lid.

"Why, there's enough gold here to make us both rich."

"True," agreed Injun Jo. He stared at the shovel in his hands. "But what's this doing here? Someone else must be looking for the treasure."

He peered around the room. Tom's heart nearly stopped beating. What if Injun Joe came up the stairs and found them both?

"Let's get away from here before anyone sees you," said the Spanish man to Injun Joe. "You are a wanted man, after all."

"Yeah," said Injun Joe. "Why don't we take the treasure with us and hide it somewhere else?"

"Where?" asked the Spanish Man.

"In the safest hiding place I know," chuckled Injun Joe. "Under the cross."

CHAPTER 5

Danger in the Cave

Tom and Huck wondered what "under the cross" meant. "They must be burying the treasure in a grave," said Tom. "Graves have crosses on them."

"Or in a disused church," said Huck, as they crept away from the house on Cardiff Hill. "I'll starts shadowing Injun Joe, Tom. He has no idea I knew his secret, too."

Back home, Tom found Aunt Polly baking a cake for the picnic the next day.

Tom had been so worried about Injun Joe, he'd forgotten all about the picnic. It was held every year for the older children in St. Petersburg. No grown-ups were allowed to go except Mr. Dobbins and a few eighteen-year-olds to organize games.

At the crack of dawn, a ferryboat full of merry children sailed down the river. It stopped at a lovely spot full of trees. Much fun was had as the children ate their picnic. Then, they played games. And soon, it was time to explore the famous McDougal's Cave.

The children all crowded around an opening in the cliffs. It was shaped like a giant "A" and it looked very dark.

"There's a guide who will show us around the cave," said Mr. Dobbins.

"You stay close to me at all times," said the guide. "Don't wander off by yourselves. The cave is like a maze, and people have been known to get lost in it. Some have never been found."

He handed out candles. The children followed him, peering in the dark. "You hold my hand, Becky," said Tom. "You don't want to get lost."

McDougal's Cave was really lots of small caves joined together with narrow tunnels. There was graffiti made with candle smoke all over the walls. Some of the children stopped to read them. "Oh,

look," said Tom.
"This one says,
'Thomas and
Gertrude were
here.' I wonder
who they were?"

Becky held up
her candle. "Did you hear that noise,
Tom? There's a waterfall in here.
Let's go see it."

"Careful! We mustn't get lost in the
dark," said Tom.

"We'll leave markers with candle smoke
on the walls," replied Becky. "That way,
we can find our way back."

They followed the noise, which led
them into a small cave. The water was
gushing out of a hole in the rocks. Next
to it was the entrance to a second tunnel.

"Oooh," said Becky. "A secret passage.
Let's see where it leads."

Before Tom could stop her, she dived
into the tunnel. Tom followed. "Becky …"

Tom's voice echoed around the walls.
Suddenly, there was a loud squeaking,
and a flock of bats appeared out of the
darkness. In a moment, the air was full of
the furry creatures flapping and diving.
One of them swooped down over Becky
and knocked the candle out of her hands.

Becky screamed. "Let's get back to the others, Tom!"

They raced down the tunnel, chased by the angry bats. But they couldn't find their way back to the waterfall. No matter how hard they tried, they kept finding themselves back where they started.

"We're lost, Becky," said Tom.

The two of them called out over and over again, but no one heard. Hours passed. Tom's candle ran out, and they found themselves in total darkness. "We're done for," cried Becky. "We're going to die in here."

"Let's stop and rest for a while," said Tom. "We don't need to panic. Your father will organize a search party when he discovers we're missing. All we have to do is wait."

Tom had some of Aunt Polly's cake in his pocket. They shared it. Becky sat with her back against a lumpy rock, and before long, she was fast asleep. Tom just sat in the darkness, thinking. Would they really be found if Judge Thatcher sent a rescue party? Would he and Becky get out alive?

Suddenly, Tom heard a noise. Footsteps. "Wake up, Becky!" he cried. "They've found us."

Lamplight glowed at the other end of the cave. Shadows moved on the cave wall. Two figures came out of a tunnel at the other end of the cave. Tom stifled a gasp.

It was Injun Joe and his Spanish friend. They were dragging something behind them, but Tom couldn't see what it was.

"I don't like this cave at night," grumbled the Spanish man. "Can't we

come back in the morning?"

"Why?" chuckled Injun Joe. "It's always dark in here no matter what time of day."

"But there are ghosts at night."

Injun Joe laughed. "Well, you go home if you're scared. I'll do this on my own."

"See you tomorrow." The Spanish man hurried off one way. Injun Joe continued the other way, dragging the heavy thing.

Tom wrapped his arms around Becky.
He was so glad she hadn't woken up.
He didn't want her to know Injun Joe was
in the cave, too. That would terrify her.

Now Tom was more determined than
ever to find a way out of the cave. He
felt in his pocket and found a ball of
kite string. He tied one end to a stone,
which he left next to the sleeping Becky.
Then, he struck out in the darkness,
leaving a trail of string behind him.
It would help him find Becky again.

Tom wandered around till the string
ran out. He was about to return to Becky
when he saw a glimmer of light. Sunlight.
He let go off the string and stumbled
toward it. The light was coming through
a hole in the rocks. It was big enough for
Tom to stick his head through.

He could see the river below. A ferryboat was chugging past.

"Help," he shouted. "Help!"

People looked up and waved. Tom was so relieved, he passed out and fell back into the darkness.

When he came around again, he was tucked up in his own bed at home, safe and sound.

CHAPTER 6

Treasure!

"How long have I been lying here, Aunt Polly?" asked Tom.

"You've been laid up for near four days," said Aunt Polly.

"And you were lost in the cave for three days," added Mary, who was cooling Tom's brow with a wet handkerchief. "Becky was very weak when we found you two. Her mother is looking after her now."

"No one will get lost in that cave again," said Judge Thatcher, who'd dropped by to check up on Tom. "I've sealed up the entrance."

"Oh, but Injun Joe is in the cave!" cried Tom.

Judge Thatcher sent some men to arrest Injun Joe at once. They found him lying on the ground, his hand stuck under the door. He had died trying to get out of the cave.

"I reckons it's fear what killed him," said Huck, when he was allowed to visit Tom.

"Injun Joe hid his treasure deep inside McDougal's Cave," Tom said to Huck when he came to visit. "I saw him dragging something out of a tunnel, and I reckon it was the treasure chest."

"Pity that the cave has been locked up," sighed Huck. "We'll never find the gold now."

"But I know a way in," replied Tom. "The same way Becky and I got out."

Aunt Polly came in to shoo Huck out of the room. But the two boys had already laid their plans. Tom waited until he heard Aunt Polly opening the door to 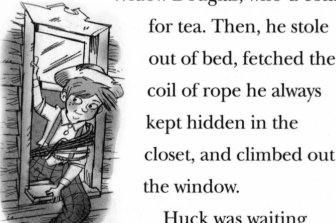Widow Douglas, who'd come for tea. Then, he stole out of bed, fetched the coil of rope he always kept hidden in the closet, and climbed out the window.

Huck was waiting at the end of the street. The two of them borrowed a raft and sailed downriver. When they got to McDougal's Cave, Tom found the hole he'd stuck his head through.

Huck tied the end of the rope to a nearby tree, and they lowered themselves in.

Huck lit a lamp that he'd brought with him. He held it up to see.

"What are we looking for, Huck?" asked Tom.

"A trail of Injun Joe's footprints," said Huck. "They'll lead us to the treasure, for sure."

"Here it is!" cried Tom. They followed the footprints till they came to a small cave.

Inside it was a small cot with a threadbare blanket on it. There was an old frying pan close by, still full of bacon rinds.

"This must have been Injun Joe's secret hideout," said Huck. "Hey, Tom, what's that on the cave wall over there?"

Tom looked at where Huck was pointing. "Why, it's a cross made with candle grease."

"Under. The. Cross," whispered Huck.

"Do you think it's the cross Injun Joe was talking about back in the haunted house?" asked Tom.

"It must be," said Huck. "We were looking for a gravestone or a church steeple, but the cross is just a marker on a wall."

The two boys approached the cross. The ground below it was rock solid.

"The treasure can't be buried here," said

Huck. "No shovel could cut through stone."

Tom knelt on the ground. "Bring the lamp closer, Huck. Do you see this large round stone? There's footprints on one side of it but not the other. That means someone stood near it and pushed it out of the way. And look, Huck, there's candle wax on the ground, same side as the footprints. Someone set a candle down here, so he could see what he was doing. I reckon the treasure is under this stone."

"Thomas Sawyer, you could be right," laughed Huck.

The two boys started pushing the stone aside. It moved slowly with a grating sound, revealing wooden boards. Tom and Huck lifted them up, and there, dark as the mouth of hell itself, was a hole in the ground.

Huck reached in. "The box is here! Help me lift it out."

They pulled up the box, and Tom threw open the lid. Gold glittered in the lamplight.

"My, but we're rich, Tom," whispered Huck in the dim light.

"Yes, we are," replied Tom. "You never need go hungry again, Huck. And you can buy yourself new clothes."

"I have no use for new clothes," said Huck. "I might be rich now, but I will stay a street boy. I will not be tamed."

The two of them dragged the chest out of the cave. It was late afternoon by the time they got to Aunt Polly's. She was fretting in the parlor. Judge Thatcher, Becky, and a few of her friends were with her. She was frantic with worry.

"I tell you, Judge, Tom's run away again."

"Huck and I went looking for treasure, Aunt Polly," said Tom through the window.

"The boy's still sick," sniffed Sid. "He's imagining things."

"But it's true," said Tom. "Huck and I brought it home in a cart we borrowed from old Benny Taylor!"

"He lives out near McDougal's Cave," added Huck.

The two boys pushed open the door and dragged the treasure chest into the parlor. Tom opened it.

"Good heavens," said Aunt Polly.

"Wow!" gasped Mary and Sid together.

"Oh, my!" Becky looked at Tom with joy in her eyes. "You're a hero, Tom!"

Tom scooped up a handful of gold. "A rich man, too, now, Becky. Come on, everyone. Ice cream is on me."